The Mermaid Who Lost Her Tiara

Cynthia Hickey

ISBN: 978-1-959788-05-8

Dedicated to Sophia, the beautiful!

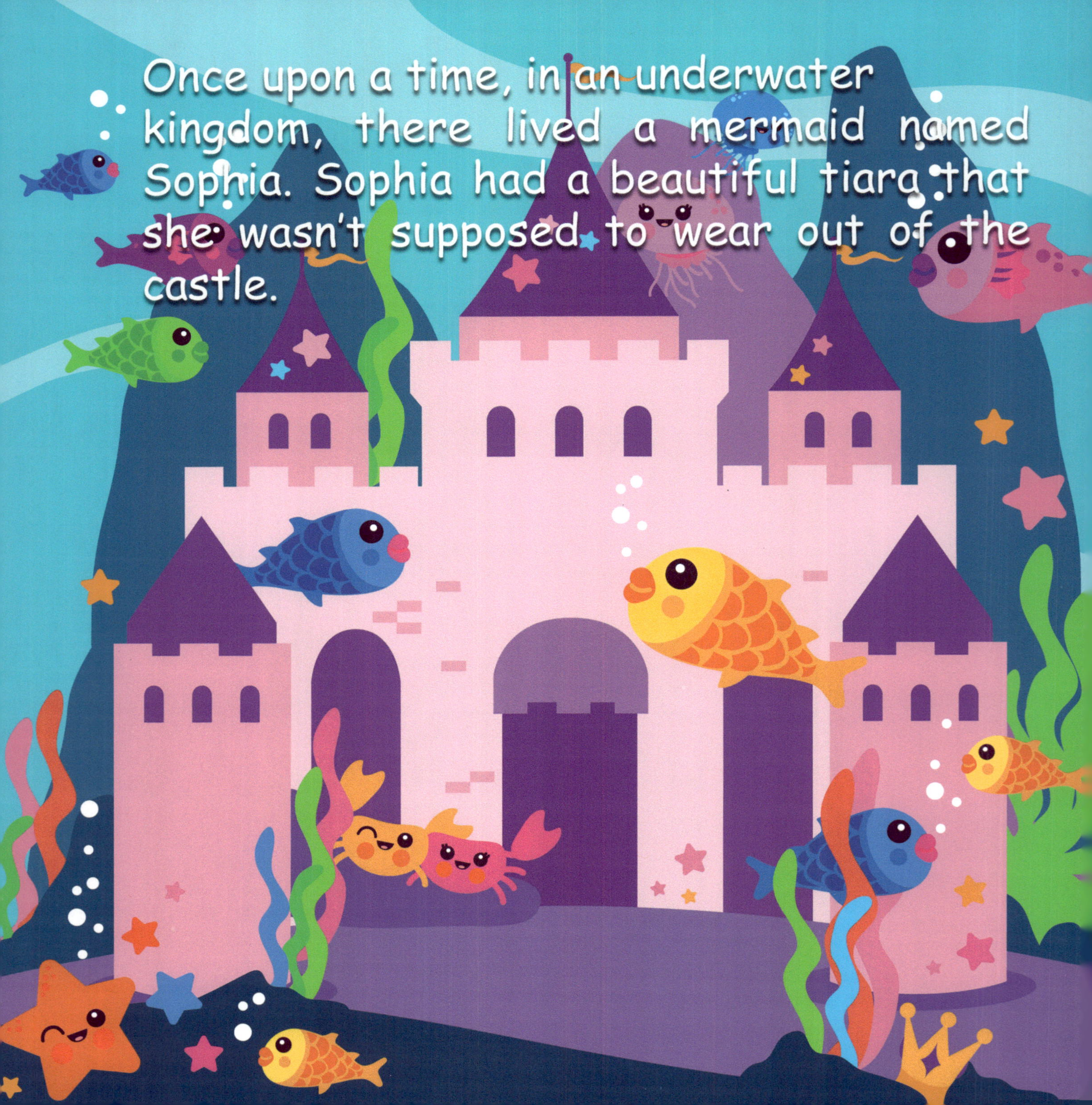
Once upon a time, in an underwater kingdom, there lived a mermaid named Sophia. Sophia had a beautiful tiara that she wasn't supposed to wear out of the castle.

The castle had a special room to hold Sophia's tiara and her mother's crown. These were only to be worn on special occasions.

But Sophia couldn't help it. The tiara made her feel pretty and special. She snuck it out of the castle every chance she got.

One day, she took it out when she went swimming with her best friend, the seal named Sally.

They went to the surface of the sea to ride the waves and do dives.

But when they leaped into the air and dived back into the sea, the tiara fell off and caught on a rock.

Sophia and Sally didn't know she'd lost the tiara and continued to play.

There was someone that wanted
Sophia's tiara. Someone who had waited
for her to lose it.

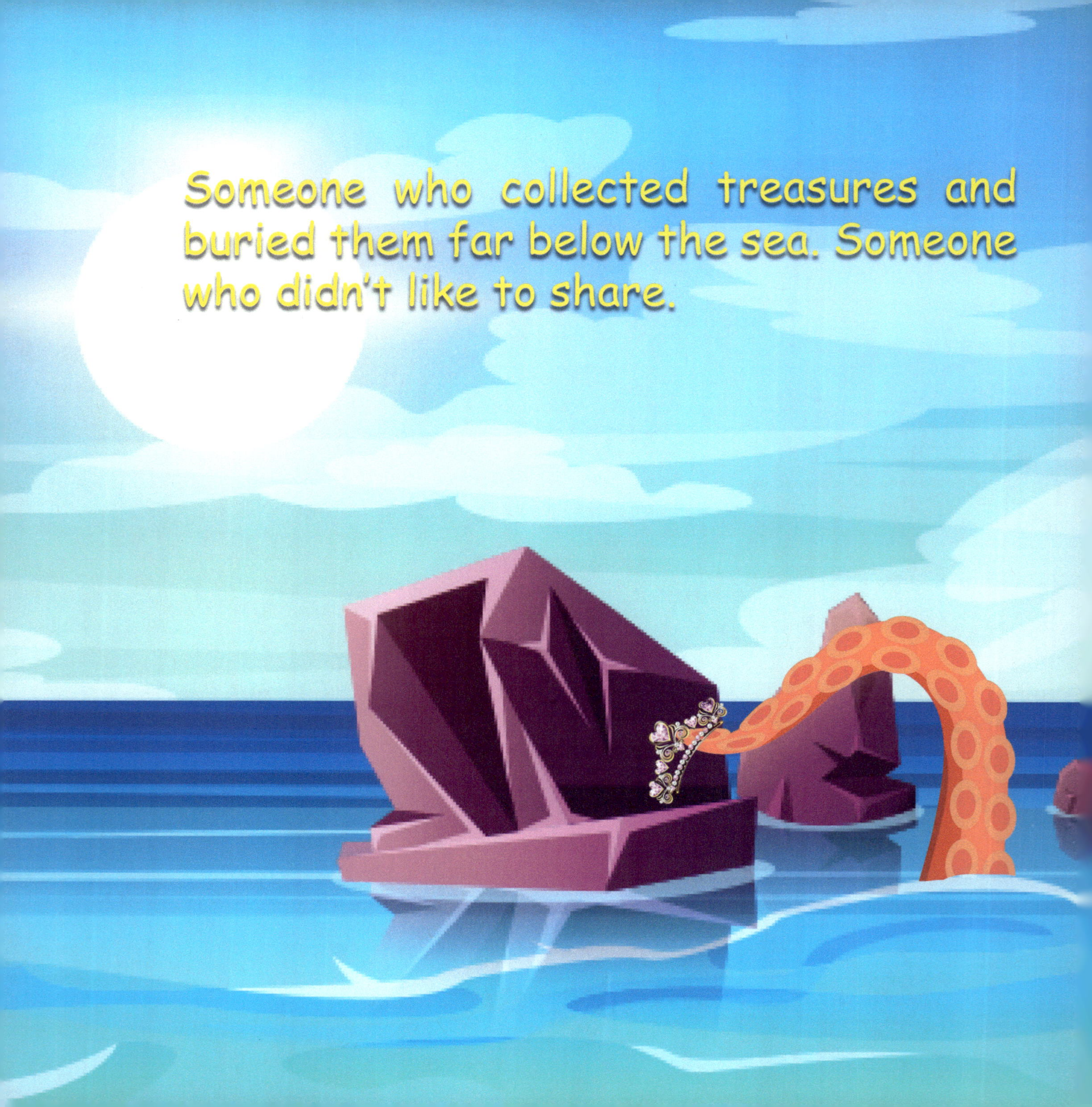
Someone who collected treasures and buried them far below the sea. Someone who didn't like to share.

Sophia and Sally went back to where they had been playing, but there was no sight of her tiara. This made Sophia very sad, because she knew her parents would be disappointed in her for disobeying them.

It was up to Sophia to find her missing tiara before her parents found out. It wouldn't be easy because night was falling and the sea got very dark at night.

"I'll be back soon," she whispered as she swam off into the night. She couldn't go home without her tiara.

Sometimes they'd find a place to stop and rest.

"What we need, Sally," Sophia said. "Is a place to spend the night until the sun shines through the water again."

"What we need," Sally replied. "Is to go home and confess to your parents that you lost your tiara."

But Sophia didn't want to. She knew her parents would ground her. She couldn't go back until she had her tiara.

The cave they found was dark and uncomfortable.

Sophia couldn't sleep with all the under the sea noises. Some fish didn't seem to go to sleep.

Especially the two arguing outside the cave.

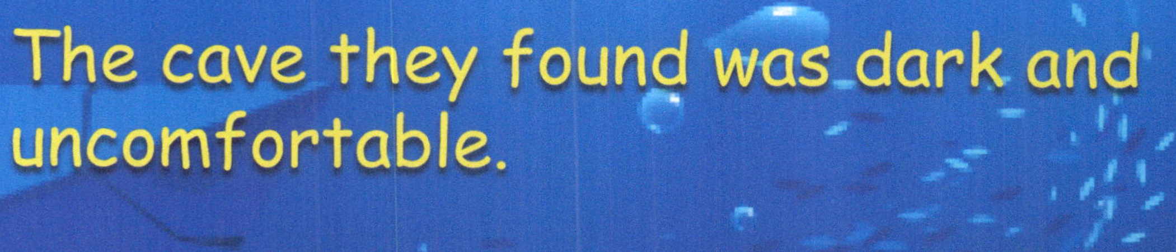

"That's what sharks do. They eat other fish."

"Break the chain," the little puffer fish said. "Just because it's always been done, doesn't mean you have to keep doing it."

And on and on they argued all through the night.

Sophia and Sally snuck out of the cave and swam carefully through a school of jelly fish.

It would hurt very much if they got stung.

Realizing how very, very lost they were, Sally suggested they look above the water to see if anything looked familiar to them.

They looked here and there and everywhere.
They couldn't see the castle or any of their
friends. They were lost!

They dove back into the sea.

The farther they swam, the bigger
and scarier things got.

But finally, the sun came out and lightened up the sea.

Sophia didn't feel quite as afraid anymore.

The farther they got from the castle, the more sea creatures they saw.

This made Sophia happy. One of them had to know where her tiara was.

She asked each and every one of them. They all said no except for a tiny, pink fish.

"I saw your tiara. A mean octopus has it hidden with his other treasures," the little fish said. "He keeps them deep in an underground cave."

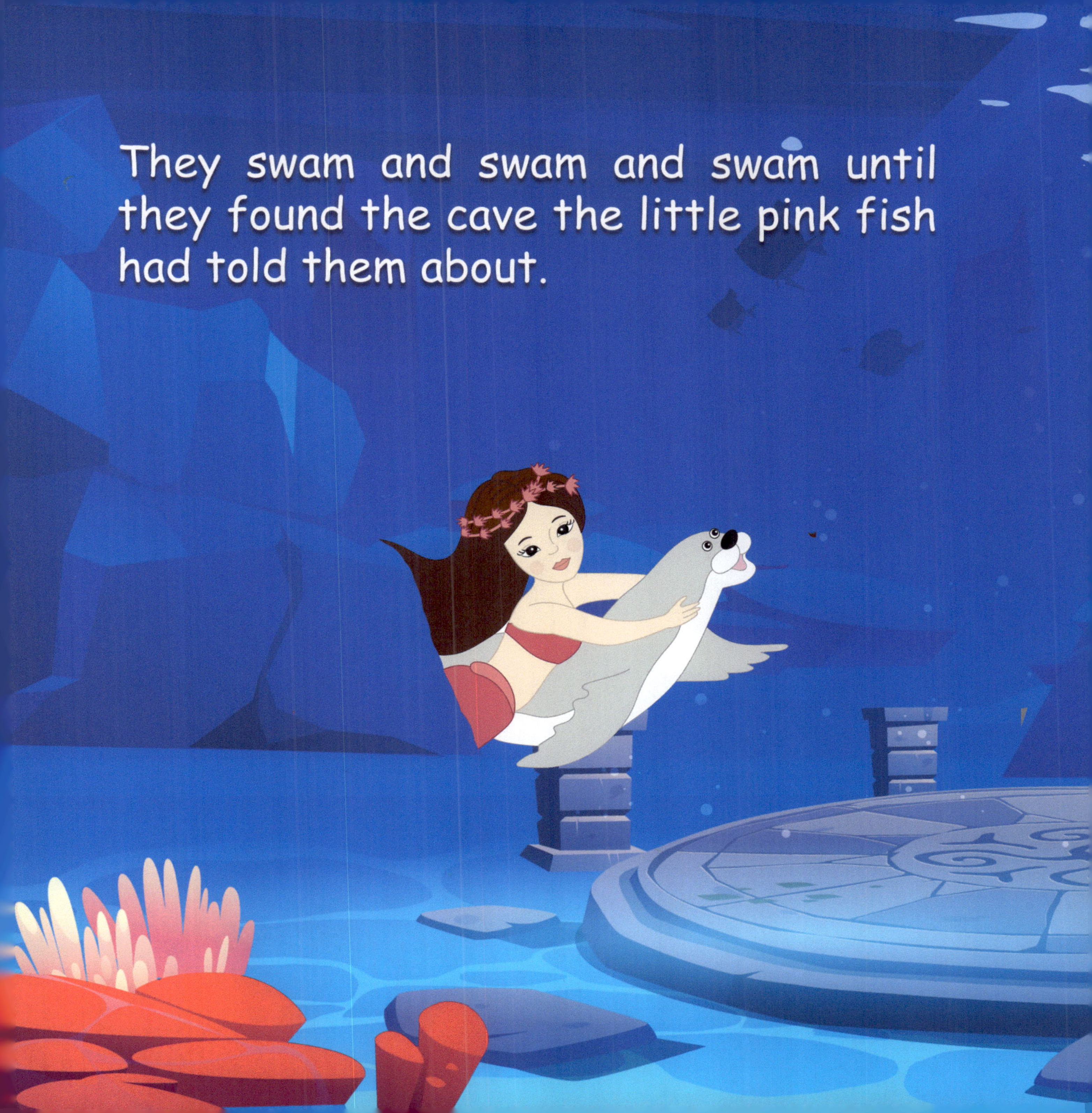

They swam and swam and swam until they found the cave the little pink fish had told them about.

As they went deeper into the cave, Sophia noticed many colored jewels littering the bottom of the ocean floor.

She collected them as they went.

There! She found the treasure chest.
And sitting on top was her tiara!

Oh, no! The mean octopus floated above the treasure chest. How could she get her tiara?

"Come closer, little mermaid. I've been following you. I believe I have something you want," the Octopus said. "But first you must give me something. I love my treasures very much and won't part with them for free."

"What could I have that you want?" Sophia asked.

"The jewels in your pocket."

"I will give them to you for the tiara and a necklace for my friend." Sophia held out her hand.

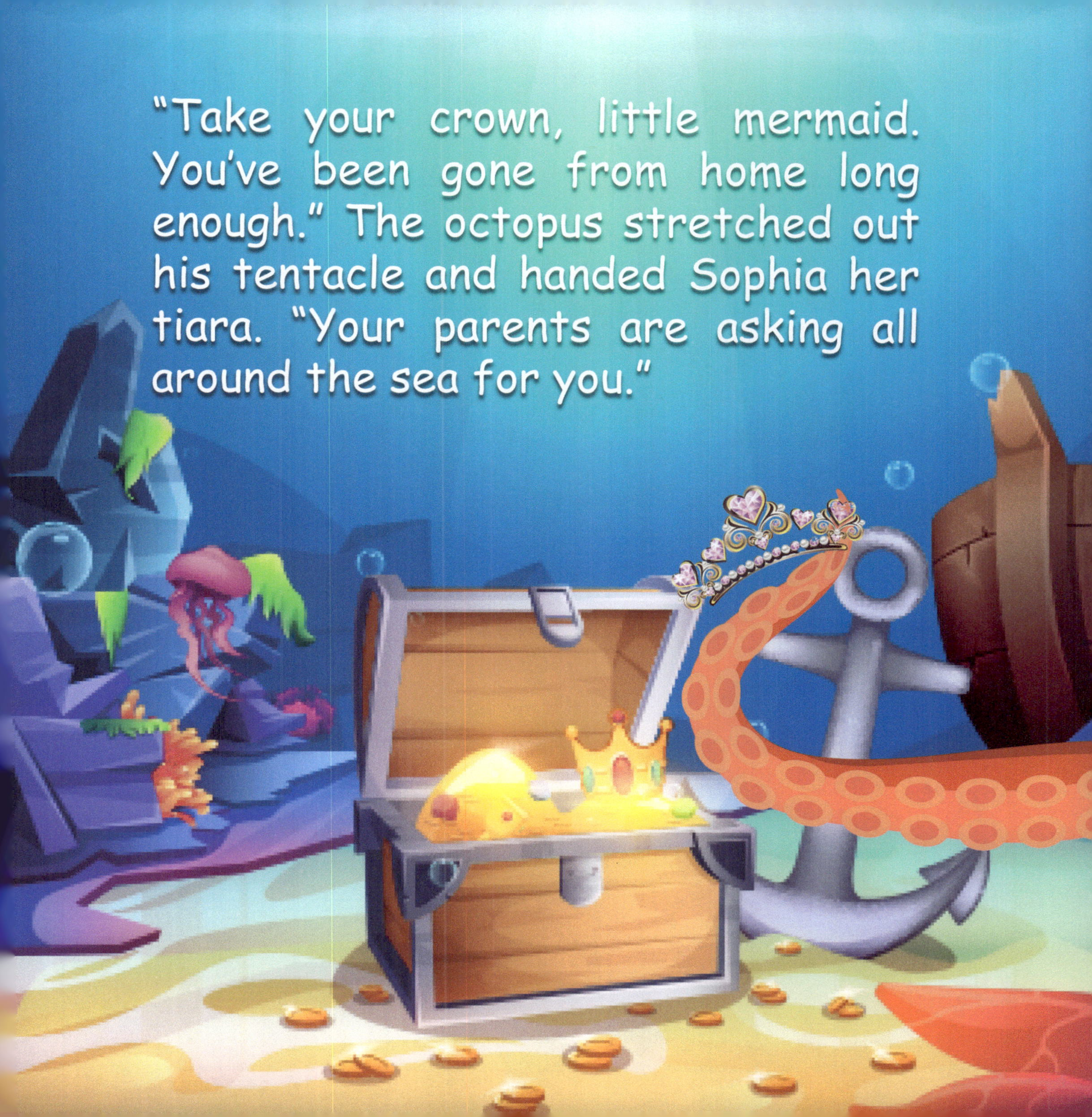

"Take your crown, little mermaid. You've been gone from home long enough." The octopus stretched out his tentacle and handed Sophia her tiara. "Your parents are asking all around the sea for you."

With Sophia wearing her tiara and Sally her new necklace, they began the long swim home.

They arrived at the castle where Sophia's parents were very disappointed, but so relieved to have their daughter home safely, they gave Sophia lots of hugs and kisses.

Sophia promised to never wear her tiara outside to play again.

Now the tiara sat back in the special room next to Sophia's Mom's crown. Right where it belonged.